FRUIT Fables

Glub Glum's Ship Flip

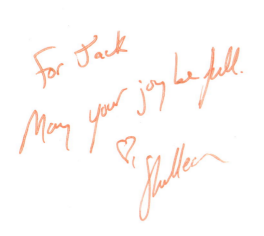

Shelleen Weaver

Haste Laud PRESS

illustrated by Cody Wood

There once was a fish named Glub Glum,
whose face was sulky and sullen.
His eyes were cast down
on ocean floor ground—
a sad and crabby old beach bum.

This fish was a bottom floor feeder–
No top-of-the-ocean snack eater.
And there he was stuck–
He wouldn't look up.
He stayed, though unhappy to be there.

One day in the depths of the ocean
arose an enormous commotion!
But Glub Glum was stuck
in mire and muck.
He had not a clue nor a notion.

A ship up above set its anchor—
a whale of an ocean oil tanker.

The anchor came down,
hit ocean floor ground,
he flipped upside down like a feather!

He lay there for just a quick minute,
and saw what the ocean had in it.
He got a good look,
said, "That's off the hook!"
then took off and started to swim it.

He saw...

Rose coral, sea horses, and clam pearls,
blue squid ink, and sunken ship vessels.
But Glub Glum liked best,
the big treasure chest
of colorful sparkly jewels!

This fish was no longer unhappy;
It wasn't the salt water taffy,
his fishhook collection,
nor other things mentioned,
but how his fins felt to be flappy!

The ship flip he had was corrective.
It made him a bit more reflective-
For joy comes to us
by looking *above*,
and gaining a higher perspective.

Let's Chew on It...

Why was Glub Glum sulky and sad in the beginning of the story?

What happened that changed Glub Glum's attitude?

Had the beautiful things around Glub Glum just appeared, or had they been there the whole time?

Glub Glum had fun collecting things on his new adventures, but where did the joy he found come from?

It must have felt scary for Glub Glum when the anchor flipped him upside down, but it turned out to be for his good. Has something new ever felt scary, but turned out to be good for you too?

We read that Glub Glum gained a higher perspective from his ship flip. What does it mean to have a higher perspective and how do we find one?

Since the word glum means "sad," the name Glub Glum doesn't fit our fish anymore. What should we call him now?

This story is about joy. Joy is one of the fruits or behaviors we learn from God's Holy Spirit. Let's say our theme verse together:

"...the fruit of the spirit is love, joy, peace, patience, kindness, goodness, faithfulness, gentleness, [and] self-control..."

— Galatians 5:22-23 NASB

Prayer:

Dear Heavenly Father,

Thank you for giving us the fruit of your Holy Spirit. Help us to have your perspective and joy. We pray in Jesus' name,
   — Amen

Dear Parents, Teachers, and Loved Ones,

Thank you for purchasing this book. Did you and your children enjoy it? I would love to hear from you. I read and respond to every email. You can contact me at: **ShelleenWeaver.com.**

There you can also find updates on my latest projects, fun freebies, and more. *Visit soon!*

Come meet us - myself and the illustrator, that is. Cody and I teamed up to bring your children a read-aloud version of this story.
We also unpack "Let's Chew On It!" and sing a theme song at the end.
Join the fun on this book's page at:
ShelleenWeaver.com.

One more thing: If you see value in this book series, would you help spread the word? Reviews are vital to authors. They help us publish and sell more books. If you purchased this book online, would you consider posting a review there? Sharing on social media or telling a friend is also very helpful. I would be grateful.

May God bless you as you train up your treasures in the way they should go.
I'm honored to be a part of your journey.

With love,

Shelleen Weaver

P.S. There's more to come in the Fruit Fables collection!
    Visit **ShelleenWeaver.com** for publishing updates.

About the Author

Shelleen Weaver is a poet, former Miss Teen of Pennsylvania, singer/songwriter/recording artist of the CRW #1 hit song, *Enraptured*, a speaker, wife, and mom...

... and completely, utterly, a child at heart.

The Fruit Fables series grew out of bedtime stories and original lullabies she told and sang to her children when they were young. Shelleen lives with her husband and three children in gorgeous Lancaster County, Pennsylvania.

More at **ShelleenWeaver.com**

About the Illustrator

Like many visual artists, Cody Wood has drawn pictures for as long as he can remember. A framed piece of his art still hangs in the elementary school of his childhood. As an animator, his work has been featured in national TV ads and on Cartoon Network. Despite a career in the visual arts, Fruit Fables is his first venture into book illustration.

Cody has also spent time as a worship leader and student ministry director. He lives in Columbus, Ohio with his wife and two sons.